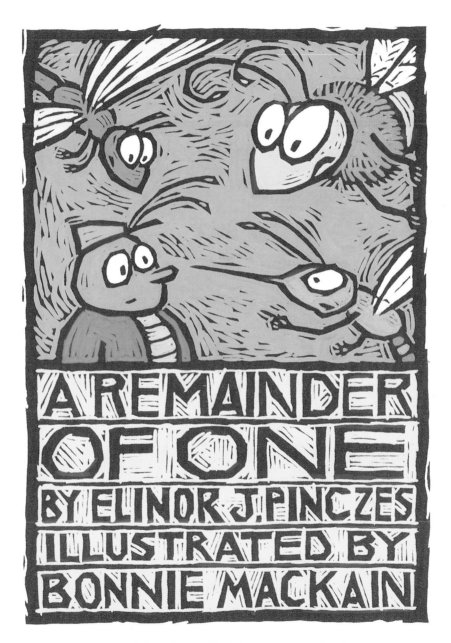

A REMAINDER OF ONE

BY ELINOR J. PINCZES

ILLUSTRATED BY

BONNIE MACKAIN

Houghton Mifflin Company Boston

To John, with love   —E.P.

For Bill   —B.S.M.

Library of Congress Cataloging-in-Publication Data

Pinczes, Elinor J.
   A remainder of one / Elinor J. Pinczes ; illustrated by Bonnie
MacKain.
      p.   cm.
   Summary: When the queen of the bugs demands that her army
march in even lines, Private Joe divides the marchers into more
and more lines so that he will not be left out of the parade.
   ISBN 0-395-69455-8
   [1. Insects—Fiction.   2. Division—Fiction.   3. Stories in
rhyme.]   I. MacKain, Bonnie, ill.   II. Title.
PZ8.3.P558676Re   1995   94-5446
[E]—dc20   CIP
                            AC

Printed in the United States of America

WOZ   10

The story of Joe might just well explain
what happens to numbers when they must remain
after division, and they're left behind
as lonesome remainders. It seems so unkind!

Down by an orchard of young apple trees
the sunshine felt hot, about 90 degrees.

So insects all scurried for any cool shade;
from mushroom or leaf, they watched a parade.

The 25th squadron marched past the bug crowd,
bound and determined to make their queen proud.

The troop had divided by two for the show.
Each bug had a partner—except soldier Joe.

"Hup, two, three, four!
We're in the 25th Army Corps.

Queen's count! Two, three!
We are the marching infantry."

The queen wasn't pleased. "We're unhappy to find
that one soldier's left at the end of a line."

A honeybee hovered above lone Joe's head.

"The queen likes things tidy," the bee sternly said.

"I'm sorry, Private," said Joe's Sergeant Steven.
"You must stand aside, so the troop will be even."
The two lines of twelve then marched neatly away,
while bug-soldier Joe had no choice but to stay.

Lone soldier Joe learned it wasn't much fun
to find himself labeled "remainder of one"!
The brainy bug-soldier stayed up the whole night.
Perhaps one more line would make everything right?

All 25 soldiers marched past the bug crowd,
nervously hoping they'd make their queen proud.

The troop had divided by three for the show;
Each line seemed perfect. Then someone spied Joe.

"Hup, two, three, four!
We're in the 25th Army Corps.

Queen's count! Two, three!
We are the marching infantry."

The regal head shook. "It's disturbing to find
one oddball bug at the end of a line."

A slender mosquito loomed over Joe's head.
"Too bad you're a misfit," the pest sharply said.

"I'm sorry, Private," said Joe's Sergeant Steven.
"If you stand aside, then the troop will look even."
The three lines of eight all marched neatly away
while sad and disheartened, poor Joe had to stay.

The oddball bug Joe knew it wasn't much fun
to feel so left out—a remainder of one.
Again the lone soldier thought all through the night.
With one more bug line, it might work out right.

The 25th squadron marched past the bug crowd,
anxiously longing to make their queen proud.

The troop had divided by four for the show.
The lines all looked even, till they spotted Joe.

Her highness pointed. "We're angry to find
a tag-along bug at the end of one line."

A shy dragonfly fluttered over Joe's head.

"Now, don't get discouraged," the fly softly said.

"I'm sorry, Private," said Joe's Sergeant Steven.
"You must stand aside, then the troop will be even."
As four lines of six marched so neatly away,
sad Joe couldn't watch, for he had to stay.

Poor tag-along Joe didn't have any fun,
always left out—a remainder of one.
But hard-thinking Joe had the answer that night:
Another bug line *must* make it work right.

The 25th squadron marched past the proud queen.
The neatest, best troopers that she'd ever seen.

Five lines of soldiers with five in each row . . .
perfect at last—and that's *counting* Joe.

"Good show!" said her grace. "Your rows are divine.
We see no remainder to ruin your line."

The troop took great pride in their skill at dividing;
Joe was pleased he was there marching, not hiding.

The coolest bug-soldier beneath the hot sun?
Smart Joe, the former remainder of one!